Coyote Concert

On A Full Moon Night

By Carol Whelihan-Scherer
Illustrations by Amy Quamme

NorthWord Press
Minnetonka, Minnesota

When the sun sat down behind the sky,
and the moon stood up for a better view,
the coyotes began to sing the songs
that their mothers and fathers knew.

They crooned with upturned faces
to the white laced moon and stars . . .
and practicing softly, they'd whisper,
rehearsing their measures and bars.

The concert was known throughout the red land,
and soon invitations were sent.
Echoed times were announced along bright canyon walls;
a nocturnal desert event . . .

The first to arrive were the snakes smooth and long,
appearing when day dressed for dark.
A pinwheel of colors in circles they'd make,
and under the rocks coil and spark.

The bats from the caverns swept low and then high,
making patterns that matched waves of sound.
Like paper doll cutouts released from a box,
waltzing with G clefs they found.

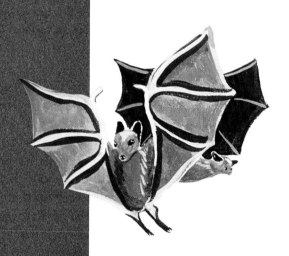

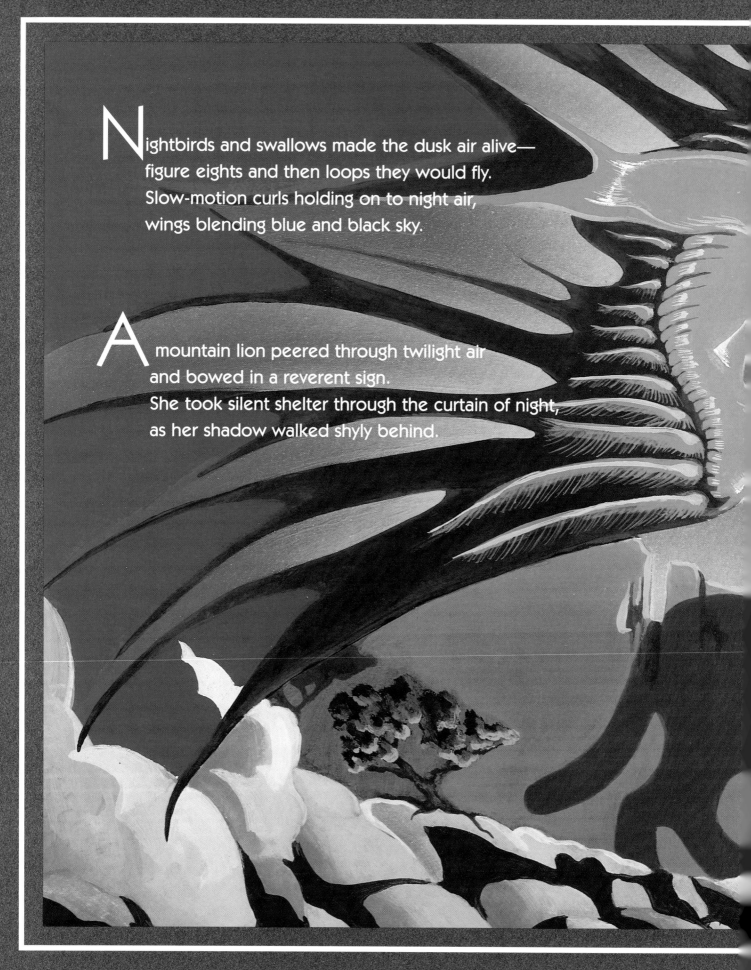

Nightbirds and swallows made the dusk air alive—
figure eights and then loops they would fly.
Slow-motion curls holding on to night air,
wings blending blue and black sky.

A mountain lion peered through twilight air
and bowed in a reverent sign.
She took silent shelter through the curtain of night,
as her shadow walked shyly behind.

Long-eared hares and road runners raced
to find the best seat in the sand.
Soon all the sprinters were resting,
softly applauding the band.

A great horned owl turned his head left and right,
then decided to perch center row.
He preened his feathers on a Joshua tree,
and settled himself for the show.

On top of an arch, a mule deer and fox
took a seat for a balcony view.
They gazed at the scene through an indigo frame,
encircling the world that they knew.

The prairie dogs popped from their homes underground
and stopped in mid-motion to hear.
They closed their eyes slowly and listened,
and knew they had nothing to fear.

The night stage was set, the moon curtain rose,
yellow and brimming with cream to the edge.
The coyotes grouped on the path by the hill
and in silence and beauty, walked up to the ledge.

One note was released by the elder—
another joined in to make two.
Soon a third, then a chorus of ages,
singing Yip, and a Roow, and an Ooooh . . .

They sang of the changing of seasons
four horsemen rode in every year.
The pups knew the lyrics from instinct,
howling so sweet and so clear.

They sang of summer and rainfall,
bringing thunder and lightning along.
Cicadas played clackers and fiddles,
winged musicians of song.

They sang of fall Aspens that glimmered,
as golden leaves covered their heads.
Squirrels used the leaves as their blankets,
as cool nights swept into their beds.

They sang of the silence of winter
whose colors were teal, clay, and white.
The snow placed caps on the boulders,
a spiraling, whispering flight.

Spring would coax warmth into winter,
as they sang of the snow melting down.
Buds and bouquets would be blooming,
each sporting a k'leidoscope crown.

The last tale was finally delivered
by a coyote, the one with no age . . .
It was sung with the knowledge and wisdom
of the coyote, the teller, the sage.

He sang of this gift that we live on—
each one has a hand in its care.
Clean water to drink, clear paths to explore,
loving thoughts gliding through purist air.

The notes stretched long on the moonbeams,
then slowly descended to ground.
They landed on prickly and saguaro
and clung to the cactus they found.

The listeners silently thanked them
and magically went with the night.
The black sky changed its face to lilac.
The sun yawned and clicked on the light.

Once more the desert was resting
after writing down memoirs in sand.
Have respect for the rights of Nature,
and nurture the life in the land.

To my special pack of "coyotes": Gregory, Genevieve, Len, Mom and Dad. Their combined spirit is always present on the pages of this full moon night; and to my sister Anne Marie, for her editorial expertise when the project was still a "pup."

Carol Whelihan-Scherer

To Mom and Dad for getting me here, and to Todd and Maddi for helping me to go further.

Amy Quamme

Book design by Russell S. Kuepper

CREATIVE
PUBLISHING
international

NorthWord Press
5900 Green Oak Drive
Minnetonka, MN 55343
1-800-328-3895

Library of Congress Cataloging-in-Publication Data
    Whelihan-Scherer, Carol,
        Coyote concert on a full moon night / by Carol Whelihan-Scherer ;
    illustrated by Amy Quamme.
            p. cm.
        Summary: At nightfall the coyotes turn up their faces and sing of changes brought by the four seasons, attracting snakes, bats, nightbirds, and other desert creatures.
        ISBN 1-55971-669-X (hardcover)
        [1. Coyotes--Fiction. 2. Desert animals--Fiction. 3. Concerts--Fiction. 4. Seasons--Fiction. 5. Stories in rhyme.] I. Quamme, Amy, ill. II. Title.
    PZ8.3.W5755 1998
    [E]--dc21
                                                                98-21783
                                                                   CIP
                                                                    AC

Printed in Malaysia